Level D

Alex Moran
Illustrated by Betsy Everitt

Green Light Readers
Harcourt, Inc.
Orlando   Austin   New York   San Diego
Toronto   London

Popcorn. Popcorn.

Put it in a pot.

Popcorn. Popcorn.

Get the pot hot.

Popcorn. Popcorn.
Put in lots more.

Popcorn. Popcorn.
One, two, three, four.

Popcorn. Popcorn.
Pop! Pop! Pop!

Popcorn. Popcorn.
Stop! Stop! Stop!

Popcorn. Popcorn.
What is the plan?

Popcorn. Popcorn.
Catch it if you can!

Popcorn. Popcorn.
It's going out the door.

Popcorn. Popcorn.
Stop! No more!

Popcorn. Popcorn.
Get it while it's hot.

We are happy.
We like it a lot!

For the Birds!

There is so much popcorn!
Why not share it with the birds?

WHAT YOU'LL NEED

 wire

 popcorn

 dried fruit

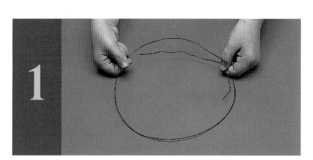

Shape the wire into a circle.

Put popcorn and fruit
on the wire.

**Twist the ends
of the wire together.**

Hang your wreath outside.

Watch for birds to come.
Keep a journal and draw pictures
of the birds you see.

Meet the Illustrator

Betsy Everitt likes to go to the movies and get a big bucket of popcorn. She and her family like to make popcorn at home, too.

For this story, Betsy Everitt chose animals with nice shapes and used lots of bright colors. She put the colors and shapes together to create feelings. How do you feel when you look at her pictures?

Dale Higgins

BETSY EVERiTT

Requests for permission to make copies of any part of the work should be mailed to the following address: Permissions Department, Harcourt, Inc., 6277 Sea Harbor Drive, Orlando, Florida 32887-6777.

www.HarcourtBooks.com

First Green Light Readers edition 1999
Green Light Readers is a trademark of Harcourt, Inc., registered in the United States of America and/or other jurisdictions.

The Library of Congress has cataloged an earlier edition as follows:
Moran, Alex.
Popcorn/Alex Moran; illustrated by Betsy Everitt.
p. cm.
"Green Light Readers."
Summary: Illustrations and rhythmic, rhyming text show what happens when popping popcorn gets out of hand.
[I. Popcorn—Fiction. 2. Stories in rhyme.]
I. Everitt, Betsy, ill. II. Title.
PZ8.3.M795Po 1999
[E]—dc21 98-15566
ISBN 0-15-204821-9
ISBN 0-15-204861-8 (pb)

A C E G H F D B
E G H F D (pb)

Ages 4-6
Grade: 1
Guided Reading Level: D
Reading Recovery Level: 6

Green Light Readers
For the reader who's ready to GO!

"A must-have for any family with a beginning reader."—*Boston Sunday Herald*

"You can't go wrong with adding several copies of these terrific books to your beginning-to-read collection."—*School Library Journal*

"A winner for the beginner."—*Booklist*

Five Tips to Help Your Child Become a Great Reader

1. Get involved. Reading aloud to and with your child is just as important as encouraging your child to read independently.

2. Be curious. Ask questions about what your child is reading.

3. Make reading fun. Allow your child to pick books on subjects that interest her or him.

4. Words are everywhere—not just in books. Practice reading signs, packages, and cereal boxes with your child.

5. Set a good example. Make sure your child sees YOU reading.

Why Green Light Readers Is the Best Series for Your New Reader

● Created exclusively for beginning readers by some of the biggest and brightest names in children's books

● Reinforces the reading skills your child is learning in school

● Encourages children to read—and finish—books by themselves

● Offers extra enrichment through fun, age-appropriate activities unique to each story

● Incorporates characteristics of the Reading Recovery program used by educators

● Developed with Harcourt School Publishers and credentialed educational consultants